MIKEY & THE MONSTER VACUUM

Text copyright © 2001 by Alysia Gonzalez
Illustrations copyright © 2001 by Joel Cook & Vuthy Kuon
All rights reserved.
Published by Providence Publishing (888) 966-3833
4306 Brook Woods, Houston, TX 77092
Printed in China through Morris Press Ltd
Third Printing 10 9 8 7 6 5 4

Library of Congress Catalog Card Number: 2001087531
Gonzalez, Alysia; Cook, Joel & Kuon,Vuthy, Mikey and the Monster Vacuum
Summary: Mikey's passion for vacuuming turns to mayhem
when he fails to listen to his mother's warning about
their new vacuum cleaner.
ISBN 0-9707906-0-0

For Michael Gabriel,
my inspiration and my joy.

A.G.

To my family, my friends at Travis and Teddy,
the best dog a boy could have.

J.C.

To Muoy, Vincent, Jonathan & Tiffanny,
I love you guys.

V.K.

ACKNOWLEDGEMENTS

*Special thanks to Vuthy for walking
with me every step of the way and
making this whole book possible.
Your vision and guidance are invaluable.*

*Thanks to Joel for the talent and
enthusiasm he has brought to this project.*

*Thanks to all the librarians, teachers and students
in the Houston area who have allowed me to
share this story with them in its infancy.*

*Thanks to Mom and Dad for always believing in me
and supporting my dream. I love you!*

*And finally, thanks to my three children,
Stephanie, Elizabeth and Michael for being patient while I
worked late hours to complete this book.
You mean the world to me.*

A.G.

MIKEY
& THE MONSTER VACUUM

story by
ALYSIA GONZALEZ

pictures by
JOEL COOK & VUTHY KUON

edited by
LAVAILLE LAVETTE

INTEGRITY PRESS, LTD.
an imprint of Hajimzel Providence Publishing

Mikey loved to vacuum.

Every morning he helped
his mother vacuum the house.

He vacuumed the carpet.
He vacuumed the curtains.
He vacuumed the couch.
He even tried to vacuum the cat!

MEOOOWWW!!

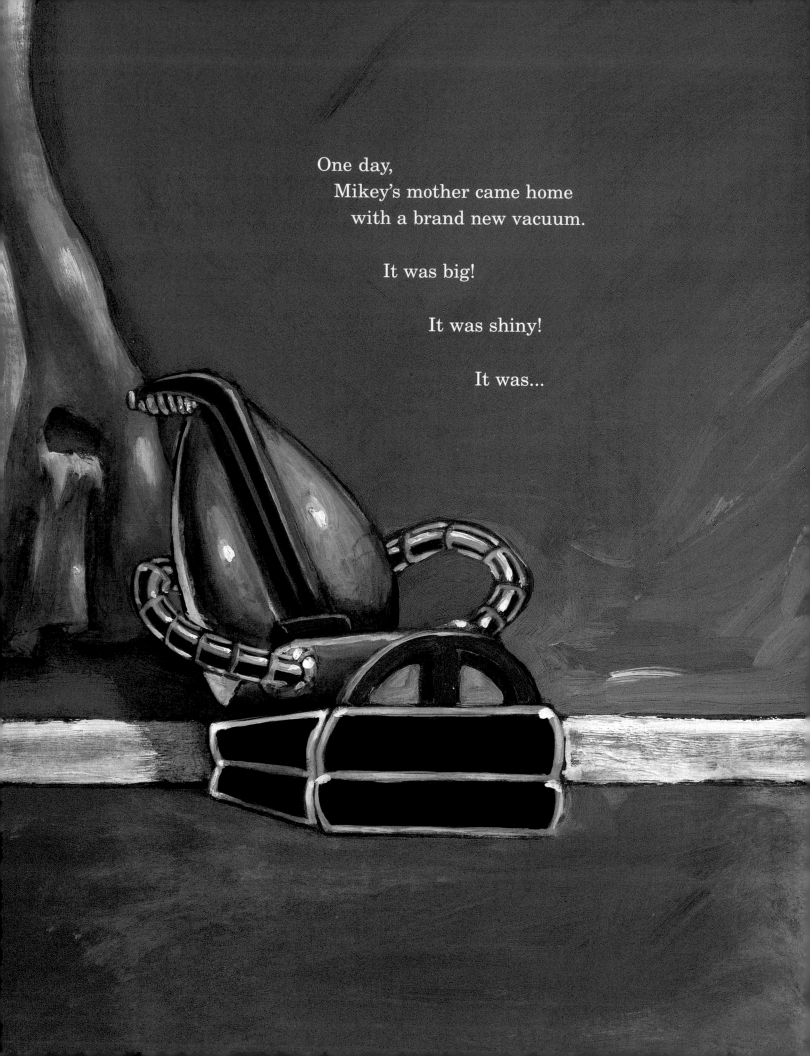

One day,
　　Mikey's mother came home
　　with a brand new vacuum.

It was big!

It was shiny!

It was...

"OFF LIMITS!"

his mother said.
"You can use the little vacuum,
but don't touch the big one."

"Yes, Momma," Mikey promised.

Mikey picked up his little vacuum.
He vacuumed the carpet.
He vacuumed the curtains.
He vacuumed the couch.
He even tried to vacuum the cat!

MEOOOWWW!!

But Mikey was no longer happy with his little vacuum.

He looked to his left.
He looked to his right.
Then he slowly tip-toed over to the
big, shiny, new vacuum cleaner.

He lifted the handle.
He flipped on the switch and...

He vacuumed the carpet.
He vacuumed the curtains.
He vacuumed the couch.
He even vacuumed UP the cat!
Sluuurrrppp!!

MEOOOWWW!!

"Uh-oh," said Mikey. "Something's not right."
The vacuum took off with him holding on tight!

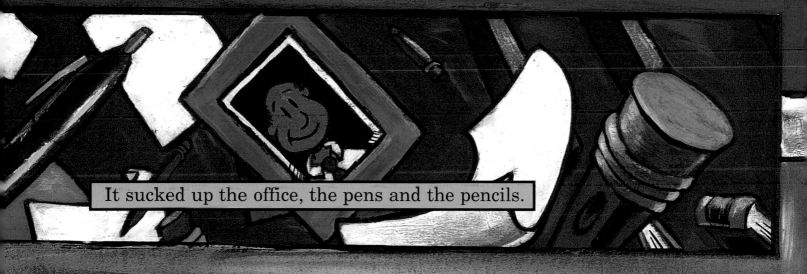

It sucked up the office, the pens and the pencils.

It sucked up the kitchen and all the utensils.

It sucked up the stairway, devoured the hall,
Then swallowed the dining room, table and ALL!

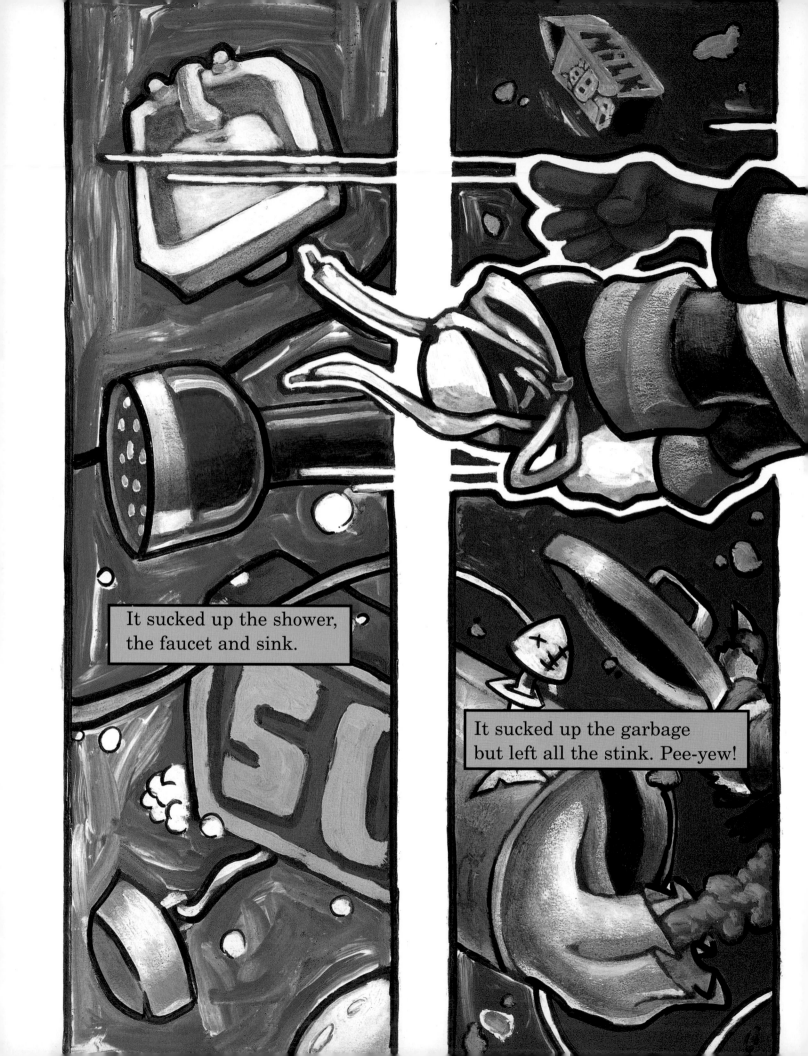

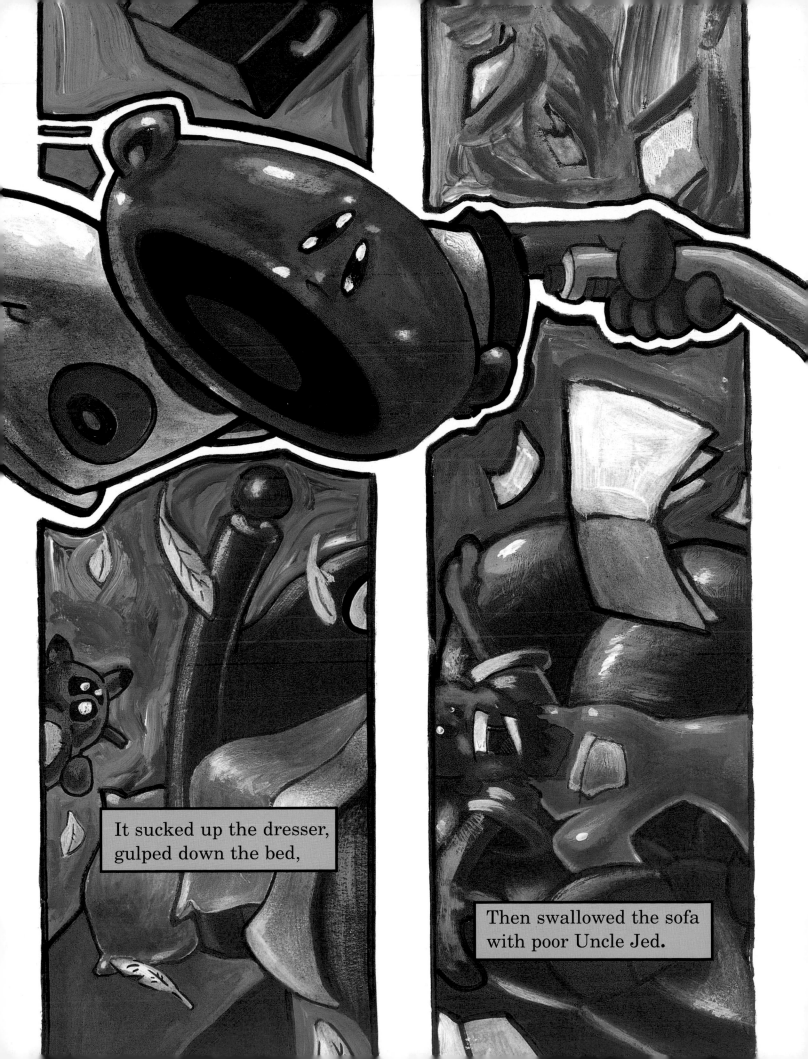

It sucked up the dresser, gulped down the bed,

Then swallowed the sofa with poor Uncle Jed.

It sucked up the salesman who knocked at the door.
He used to sell vacuums, but not anymore.
It sucked up the neighbor, his kids and his spouse.
It sucked up the mailbox and then the WHOLE house!

A few moments later
with all the dust clear,
Mikey looked up—
his momma was here!

Momma said, "Mikey,
now what did you do?"

The vacuum growled loudly
and sucked her up too!

The vacuum approached with its mouth gaping wide. Then Mikey caught sight of his momma inside!

Determined to save her, with all he could muster, He reached back and pulled out a large feather duster!

He shook up the feathers, the dust grew and grew. The vacuum replied with a thunderous...

...A-CHOO

The office blew out, then the kitchen and bed,
The shower, the garbage and poor Uncle Jed.
Then out came the neighbors one after another,
The salesman, the sofa, and finally, his mother!

"Hip, hip, hooray!" he heard them all cheer.
Mikey grinned from ear to ear.
With Mikey the Hero all covered in grime,
The battle was over and so was the rhyme.

Mikey ran to his mother.
He hugged her tight.
He was happy.
He was exhausted.
He was...

"STILL RESPONSIBLE,"

his mother said,
"for cleaning up the mess!"

"Yes, Momma," said Mikey,
reaching for his little vacuum.
But instead, his mother handed him...

...a dust pan and broom!

He swept the carpet.
He swept the curtains.
He swept the couch.
He even tried to sweep the...

MEOOOWWW!!

Author's Note

From the time my son Michael was three years old, his favorite thing to do was to vacuum the carpet. Every day he asked if he could vacuum the floor. In fact, he loved vacuuming so much that every time he went to a friend's house or to Grandma's he would ask to vacuum their carpet as well, and they usually let him. For Michael it was pure fun! That Christmas I bought him his very own little vacuum and it instantly became his favorite toy. He has been a vacuuming monster ever since.

Mikey's character and his true-life antics were the inspiration for writing this book. In the end, he learns that even a hero has to be responsible for his own choices and actions.

I have had so much fun working on this book! I appreciate the opportunity to share with you a part of my life and hope that you enjoy reading this story as much as I have enjoyed creating it.

–Alysia Gonzalez